Zinc
ALLOY

SUPER ZERO

Librarian Reviewer
Katharine Kan
Graphic novel reviewer and Library Consultant, Panama City, FL
MLS in Library and Information Studies, University of Hawaii at
Manoa, HI

Reading Consultant
Elizabeth Stedem
Educator/Consultant, Colorado Springs, CO
MA in Elementary Education, University of Denver, CO

STONE ARCH BOOKS
www.stonearchbooks.com

Graphic Sparks are published by Stone Arch Books
151 Good Counsel Drive, P.O. Box 669
Mankato, Minnesota 56002
www.stonearchbooks.com

Library of Congress Cataloging-in-Publication Data
Lemke, Donald B.
    Super Zero / by Donald Lemke; illustrated by Douglas Holgate.
    p. cm. — (Graphic Sparks. Zinc Alloy)
    ISBN 978-1-4342-0762-3 (library binding)
    ISBN 978-1-4342-0858-3 (pbk.)
    1. Graphic novels. [1. Graphic novels. 2. Heroes—Fiction. 3. Robots—Fiction.
4. Bullies—Fiction.] I. Holgate, Douglas ill. II. Title.
PZ7.7.L33Su 2009
[Fic]—dc22   2008006712

Summary: Zack Allen loves comic books, but he's nothing like his favorite superheroes.
He's always getting picked on by bullies at school. Then one day, Zack builds a high-tech
robot suit. Now he must decide how to use his newfound powers. He has become Zinc
Alloy, the world's newest superhero!

Art Director: Heather Kindseth
Graphic Designer: Brann Garvey

1 2 3 4 5 6 13 12 11 10 09 08

Printed in the United States of America

Zinc ALLOY

SUPER ZERO

by Donald Lemke   illustrated by Douglas Holgate

Zinc Alloy

Johnny   Billy

7

The next morning . . .

I hope you didn't spend all night reading comics, son.

Of course not, Dad.

I was working on, uh, a little science project. Heehee!

Zack imagined the fun he would have scaring the bullies in his robot suit.

ROCKET POPS!

But then . . .

BREAKING NEWS!

Breaking news!

A runaway train continues to circle the tracks in downtown Metro City . . .

MUNCH

MUNCH

MUNCH

Its brakes are not working, and it cannot be stopped!

BREAKING NE

Dozens of frightened passengers remain trapped onboard, suffering from severe motion sickness!

Zack?

MUNCH!

About the Author

Growing up in a small Minnesota town, Donald Lemke kept himself busy reading anything from comic books to classic novels. Today, Lemke works as a children's book editor and pursues a master's degree in publishing from Hamline University in St. Paul, Minnesota. Lemke has written a variety of children's books and graphic novels. His ideas often come to him while running along the inspiring trails near his home.

About the Illustrator

Douglas Holgate is a freelance illustrator from Melbourne, Australia. His work has been published all around the world by Random House, Simon and Schuster, the *New Yorker* magazine, and Image Comics. His award-winning comic "Laika" appears in the acclaimed comic collection *Flight, Volume Two.*

Glossary

alloy (AL-oi)—a mixture of two or more types of metal

clumsy (KLUHM-zee)—careless or awkward in the way a person walks or moves

construct (kuhn-STRUHKT)—to make or build something

flexibility (flek-suh-BIL-ih-tee)—the ability to bend and change shape

noogie (NOO-gee)—rubbing one's knuckles on a person's head for a slightly painful form of torture

revealed (ri-VEE-uhld)—to make something known, such as telling a secret

rocket booster (ROK-it BOO-stur)—a special rocket that gives extra power to a spacecraft

wet willie (WET WIHL-ee)—to lick one's finger and then shove it into another person's ear

zinc (ZINGK)—a blue-white metal used in many alloys; iron and steel are often coated with zinc to keep them from rusting

History of COMICS

Did you know the first comics are more than 30,000 years old? That's right! In Lascaux, France, early humans carved and painted images of animals onto cave walls. Many people believe these are the first "comic" stories.

About 5,000 years ago ancient Egyptians used pictures and symbols, called hieroglyphs (HYE-ur-uh-glifs), to tell stories about their people and culture. Many of these tales can still be seen on the walls of Egypt's pyramids.

In 1754, Benjamin Franklin created the first cartoon published in an American newspaper. The cartoon showed a snake cut into eight pieces with the words "Join, or Die." Instead of being funny, Franklin hoped the comic would help unite the eight American colonies.

In 1897, R. F. Outcault created "The Yellow Kid," which many believe is the first comic strip. In the strip, Outcault used the first ever word balloon. Word balloons are the bubbles filled with the text of a character's spoken words.

In the early 1900s, comics and cartoons became more popular with children. In November 1928, Walt Disney released a short animated film called "Steamboat Willie." It was the first Mickey Mouse cartoon to have sound.

The first issue of *Action Comics* was released in June 1938. The issue contained the first appearance of Superman, a character created by Jerry Siegel and Joe Shuster.

Many people use the term "graphic novel" to describe a series of short comics collected into a longer book. In 1978, Will Eisner's *A Contract with God* was the first book to label itself a graphic novel.

Today, many artists publish comics and graphic novels on the Internet. In 2004, Jeff Kinney started an original web book called *Diary of a Wimpy Kid*. In 2007, the book was published and became a *New York Times* best seller.

Discussion Questions

1. Instead of getting back at the bullies, Zack Allen chose to stop the runaway train. Why do you think he decided to use the Zinc Alloy suit for good instead of evil? Would you have made the same decision? Explain.

2. Each page of a graphic novel has several illustrations called panels. What is your favorite panel in this book? Describe what you like about the illustration and why it's your favorite.

3. *Robo Hero* is Zack Allen's favorite comic book. What is your favorite comic book or superhero? Describe why you like that book or character the best.

Writing Prompts

1. Imagine Zack Allen loaned you his Zinc Alloy suit for 24 hours. Write a story about your adventures. What would you do in the suit? Where would you go?

2. At the end of the story, the author hints that Zack will use the Zinc Alloy suit again. Write your own Zinc Alloy book. Who will he have to save next?

3. Many comic books are written and illustrated by two different people. Write a story, and then give it to a friend to illustrate.

Internet Sites

The book may be over, but the adventure is just beginning.

Do you want to read more about the subjects or ideas in this book? Want to play cool games or watch videos about the authors who write these books? Then go to FactHound. At *www.facthound.com*, you'll be able to do all that, and more. The FactHound website can also send you to other safe Internet sites.

Check it out!